Collecting Data in Animal Investigations

Diana Noonan

Real World Math Books are published by Capstone Press,
151 Good Counsel Drive, P.O. Box 669, Mankato, Minnesota 56002.
www.capstonepub.com

032010
005740CGF10

Books published by Capstone Press are manufactured with paper
containing at least 10 percent post-consumer waste.

Library of Congress Cataloging-in-Publication Data
Noonan, Diana.
  Collecting data in animal investigations / by Diana Noonan.—1st hardcover ed.
    p. cm. — (Real world math level 4)
  Includes index.
  ISBN 978-1-4296-5237-7 (library binding)
  1. Animals—Juvenile literature. 2. Animal ecology—Juvenile
literature. 3. Ecology—Methodology—Juvenile literature. I. Title.
II. Series.
  QL49.N636 2011
  590.72'3—dc22   2010001816

Editorial Credits

Sara Johnson, editor; Emily R. Smith, M.A.Ed., editorial director; Sharon Coan, M.S.Ed., editor-in-chief;
Lee Aucoin, creative director; Rachelle Cracchiolo, M.S.Ed., publisher

Photo Credits

The author and publisher would like to gratefully credit or acknowledge the following for permission
to reproduce copyright material: cover BigStockPhoto.com; p.4 istockphoto; p.5 Shutterstock; p.8
Shutterstock; p.10 BigStockPhoto.com; p.12 Alamy; p.13 Shutterstock; p.15 (main) Shutterstock; p.15
(inset) BigStockPhoto.com; p.16 Alamy; p.17 (top left) Shutterstock; p.17 (top right) Shutterstock;
p.17 (bottom) Photolibrary.com; p.18 istockphoto; p.19 BigStockPhoto.com; p.20 Alamy; p.21 (left)
Shutterstock; p.21 (right) Alamy; p.22 Science Photo Library; p.23 istockphoto; p.24 Alamy; p.25 Science
Photo Library; p.27 istockphoto; p.29 Alamy. Illustrations on pp. 6, 7,11, 14, 21, 23, and 24 by Xiangyi Mo.

While every care has been taken to trace and acknowledge copyright, the publishers tender their
apologies for any accidental infringement where copyright has proved untraceable. They would be
pleased to come to a suitable arrangement with the rightful owner in each case.

Table of Contents

Animals in the City 4

Dragonflies 6

Honeybees 8

Mallard Ducks 9

Sparrows 10

Rabbits 11

Chipmunks 12

Predictions at the Park 13

Dragonfly Prediction 15

Honeybee and Duck Predictions 17

Sparrow Prediction 18

Rabbit Prediction 19

Chipmunk Prediction 20

Accurate Predictions 21

One Last Prediction 27

Problem-Solving Activity 28

Glossary 30

Index 31

Answer Key 32

Animals in the City

Mr. Martin's fourth grade class is learning about animals that live in the city. Mr. Martin says that they will go to City Park on Friday this week. They will try to find the animals they have learned about.

LET'S EXPLORE MATH

Mr. Martin's class draws a chart showing the weather **predictions** for the week that they are going to City Park. They do this so they will know what types of clothing to wear on Friday.

Weather This Week

Day of the Week	Temperature
Monday	68°F
Tuesday	64°F
Wednesday	66°F
Thursday	70°F
Friday	76°F

Use the table above to answer these questions.

a. Which days have a predicted temperature of 70°F or more?

b. Based on the predictions, how many degrees warmer will Friday be than Monday?

The class is divided into teams of six. The Wildlife Trackers team is Luis, Marcy, Todd, Emily, Sheng, and Afua. They have 6 animals to study: dragonfly, honeybee, mallard (MAL-ard) duck, sparrow, rabbit, and chipmunk.

Learning about Learning!

The Wildlife Trackers team needs to do research. Research means to study and investigate something. Then the team needs to collect **data**. The data can be put together in many ways.

Dragonflies

Marcy uses the Internet to find data on dragonflies. Dragonflies are insects. They have 3 parts to their bodies. All dragonflies have 4 long wings.

Adult dragonflies lay eggs in water or on plants over water. And some dragonflies lay their eggs in mud at the edge of water.

First, Marcy makes a **diagram** to show the information she found.

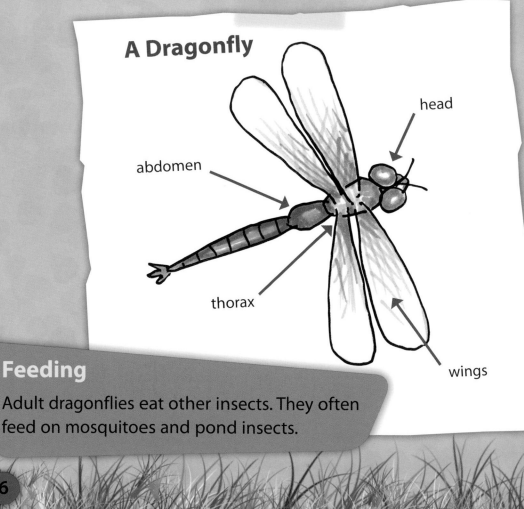

A Dragonfly

head

abdomen

thorax

wings

Feeding

Adult dragonflies eat other insects. They often feed on mosquitoes and pond insects.

Dragonfly Nymphs

Next, Marcy learns that young dragonflies are called nymphs (NIMPFZ). Nymphs have small wings and cannot fly. But they have gills to breathe in water. Fish eat young dragonflies. Marcy then makes a dragonfly **life cycle** chart.

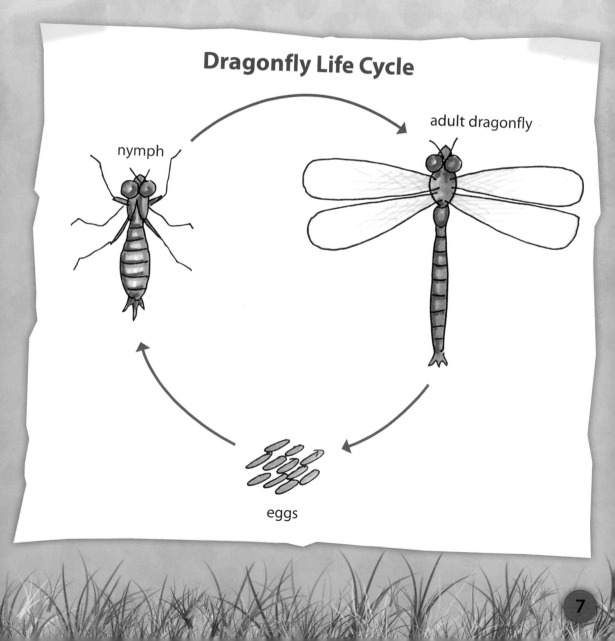

Dragonfly Life Cycle

nymph

adult dragonfly

eggs

Honeybees

Afua also learns about an insect. She learns about the honeybee. Afua sends an e-mail with questions to an **entomologist** (en-tuh-MOL-uh-jist). Then Afua uses a star diagram to **record** her information.

A Honeybee

Bees have long tongues. They use their tongues to collect pollen and nectar from flowers.

Bees are insects.

Bees store flower pollen in pollen sacks on their legs.

Bees use the sun to help them find their way.

Bees visit hundreds of flowers each day.

Mallard Ducks

Todd reads books to learn about the mallard duck. Then he makes a chart. He collects his information under different headings.

The Mallard Duck

beak	wide with rounded tip, used for scooping and eating from soft ground
legs	short (mallard ducks waddle)
feet	webbed to help duck swim
food	seed (e.g., corn, barley, wheat), small fish, tadpoles, freshwater snails

LET'S EXPLORE MATH

Todd also reads about mallard duck eggs. He learns that a mallard duck lays between 9 and 13 eggs each breeding season. This table shows how many eggs were laid each year over 4 years by a mallard duck.

Mallard Duck Eggs

Year	Year 1	Year 2	Year 3	Year 4
Eggs laid	9	12	11	10

a. What is the total number of eggs the mallard duck laid?

b. Draw a bar graph to show the data.

Sparrows

Luis studies sparrows. He asks his uncle for help. Uncle Marco is a bird watcher. He gives Luis some sparrow facts. Then Luis makes a list of those facts.

Sparrow Facts

1. Sparrows have short, blunt beaks to help them eat seeds and grains.
2. Sparrows also eat bugs and household scraps.
3. A sparrow's claws help it hold tight to small branches.
4. Sparrows feed together in flocks.

LET'S EXPLORE MATH

At home, Luis counts how many sparrows he sees every day for a week. On Monday Luis sees 1 sparrow, on Tuesday he sees 3, on Wednesday he sees 4, on Thursday he sees 3, on Friday he sees 2, on Saturday he sees 6, and on Sunday he sees 7.

Create a **frequency table** for this information, in order of most sparrows seen to least sparrows seen.

Rabbits

Sheng and Emily are both studying **mammals**. Sheng learns about rabbits on the Internet. He records his information in a diagram.

A Rabbit

long ears help rabbits hear danger

white tail flashes to warn other rabbits of danger

strong front teeth for nibbling grass

strong front legs for digging **burrows** in soil

long back legs for hopping

Chipmunks

Emily learns about chipmunks by calling a City Park **ranger**. Emily records what the ranger tells her. Then Emily makes a list of facts.

Chipmunk Facts

1. Chipmunks eat nuts, seeds, berries, and insects.
2. They carry food in pouches in their cheeks.
3. They have five toes on each foot.
4. Sharp claws help chipmunks climb trees.
5. They use their sharp claws to dig burrows beneath trees.

Predictions at the Park

Mr. Martin is very pleased with the data collected. On Friday, he takes the class and some parent helpers to City Park.

"Bring your animal diagrams and charts," he says.

"And our sun hats, too," says Marcy. "Hot, sunny weather is predicted."

Mr. Martin gives everyone a map of the park. He asks each child to study the park map.

"Can you predict where in the park you might find your animal?" he asks.

City Park

woods

playground

meadow

stream

flower garden

wetlands

fish pond

picnic area

Dragonfly Prediction

"I know where my dragonfly adults and nymphs live," says Marcy. "They will be at the fish pond. Adult dragonflies lay their eggs close to water. And the nymphs live in the water."

"It is possible that you will find them at the fish pond," says Mr. Martin. "But it is even more **probable** that you will find plenty of nymphs in the wetlands. Why is that?"

Marcy thinks hard. She looks back through her data. "Fish eat dragonfly nymphs," she says. "So it is more probable that I would find nymphs in the wetlands. There is water there but it is too shallow for fish to live in."

"Good thinking!" says Mr. Martin.

a dragonfly nymph

LET'S EXPLORE MATH

Marcy finds dragonfly nymphs at the pond and at the wetlands. She puts her data in a table.

Number of Dragonfly Nymphs Found

	At the Pond	At the Wetlands
Nymphs	8	29

Draw a bar graph to show this data.

Honeybee and Duck Predictions

Afua looks at the park map. Then she looks over her data. She reads that bees collect pollen and nectar from flowers.

"I'm going to look in the flower garden for bees!" she says.

Todd reads through his data on mallard ducks. They have webbed feet for swimming. They eat water snails, tadpoles, and small fish. Where do you think Todd will find mallard ducks?

Sparrow Prediction

Luis looks over his data on sparrows.

"Sparrows are tricky," he says to Mr. Martin. "They eat grass seeds. It is probable that they will be in the meadow. They also like eating scraps. So it is also probable they will be in the picnic area!"

"You might have to go to a few places," says Mr. Martin.

Rabbit Prediction

Sheng looks at his data. Rabbits eat grass. They dig burrows. They also use their tails to warn each other about danger. So they need to live in open areas.

Your Turn to Predict!

Look back at Sheng's data on rabbits. Where do you think it is probable that Sheng will find rabbits? Where is it not probable?

Chipmunk Prediction

Emily looks at her chipmunk data. Then she studies the map. Chipmunks have sharp claws to climb trees. They also use their claws to dig burrows.

"It is not very probable that I would find them in the flower garden," she says. "But it is highly probable that I would see some chipmunks if I went to the woods."

The City Park ranger had also sent Emily this bar graph. It shows the number of male, female, and baby chipmunks living in City Park. Which type of chipmunk will Emily probably see the most?

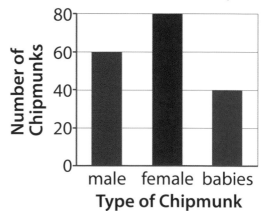

Chipmunks in City Park

Number of Chipmunks / Type of Chipmunk

male female babies

Accurate Predictions

At noon, everyone meets at the picnic area for lunch. "Were your predictions **accurate**?" asks Mr. Martin.

"Yes!" says Marcy. "I found dragonflies and nymphs in the wetlands."

"Good work," says Mr. Martin.

"And I found plenty of bees in the flower garden," says Afua.

"Sheng didn't see any rabbits," says a parent. "But he was right in his predictions about where to look for them."

"There were rabbit burrows all along the banks of the stream," says Sheng. "The rabbits must find it easy to dig in the soft soil there."

Dusk and Dawn

Rabbits feed at dusk and early in the morning. If Mr. Martin's class stays late at the park, Sheng will probably see rabbits.

"I thought it was probable that the sparrows would be in most places," says Luis. "And I was right! They were in the meadow. They were also in the picnic area. And I saw them in the flower garden, too. They were looking for insects. I got some great photos of them."

"Good predicting," says Mr. Martin.

Photographs are another great way of collecting and showing data.

"We found the chipmunks," says Emily. "They were exactly where I had predicted we would find them. They were in the woods. I saw them on the ground and in the trees."

"Well," says Mr. Martin, "now it is Todd's turn. Todd has a very interesting story to tell us about his mallard ducks."

"I do," says Todd. "I predicted that I would find them at the pond and the wetlands. I did not think it was probable that they would be anywhere else. So I went to the wetlands and the pond. But I only saw 2 ducks at the pond. The rest were gone!"

"And where did you find them?" asks Mr. Martin.

Male mallard ducks have beautiful green heads. Female mallard ducks are mostly brown in color.

A New Prediction

Look back at the map on page 14. Can you think where else the ducks might be?

"All the ducks were here, in the picnic area," says Todd. "A family was feeding them sandwiches. Ducks must like sandwiches more than snails!"

"I guess even the best predictions are not always accurate," smiles Mr. Martin.

Everyone laughs but not for long.

The next week, Todd makes a bar graph to show the number of ducks he found in different parts of the park.

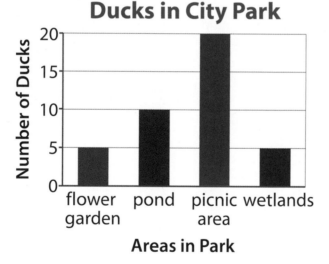

Look at the graph and answer the questions.

a. Which 2 areas have the same number of ducks?

b. How many more ducks are there in the picnic area than in the pond?

c. How many ducks does Todd see altogether?

One Last Prediction

"Oh, no!" says Mr. Martin. "Here come the ducks again!"

"I have one last prediction," says Todd. "The ducks are coming for our sandwiches!"

Save the Birds!

Jacinta has a flowering dogwood tree in her backyard. She loves to watch the beautiful birds that come to eat the berries. Her neighbor, Mr. Hodges, wants Jacinta to cut down the tree because the berries are falling into his garden.

Jacinta knows Mr. Hodges also likes watching birds. She decides to count the number of birds so she can create a graph that shows how many birds would not visit their yards if she cut the tree down. She thinks this will convince Mr. Hodges to let her keep the tree.

Birds in the Tree

Day of the Week	Number of Birds
Monday	||||| ||||| ||||| ||
Tuesday	||||| ||||| ||||| ||||
Wednesday	||||| ||||| ||||| |||||
Thursday	||||| ||||| ||||| |||
Friday	||||| ||||| ||||| ||||| ||
Saturday	||||| ||||| ||||| ||
Sunday	||||| ||||| |||||	

Solve It!

a. Draw a frequency table to show the number of birds (in numerals) that visit the tree each day for the week.

b. Use the data in the table to draw the graph that Jacinta creates to show Mr. Hodges.

c. Write 3 questions about the graph.

Glossary

accurate—correct

burrows—holes in the ground that rabbits and chipmunks live in

data—information gathered for experiments or projects

diagram—a simple drawing that explains or shows something

entomologist—a scientist who studies insects

frequency table—a chart that shows a set of events and how often the events occur

life cycle—the changes a living thing goes through from the start of its life to its adult form and then to its death

mammals—animals whose babies feed on milk from their mothers

predictions—things that are said to happen in the future based on observations and experiences

probable—expected to happen or be true

ranger—a person whose job it is to look after a park or public area

record—to write down information

Index

chipmunk, 5, 12, 20, 24

City Park, 4, 12, 13–14, 20, 26

diagram, 6, 8, 11, 13

dragonfly, 5, 6–7, 15–16, 21

entomologist, 8

honeybee, 5, 8, 17, 21

insects, 6, 8, 23

Internet, 6, 11

life cycle, 7

mallard duck, 5, 9, 17, 24, 25, 26, 27

mammals, 11

nymphs, 7, 15–16

pollen, 8, 17

rabbit, 5, 11, 19, 22

sparrow, 5, 10, 18, 23

weather, 4, 13

Let's Explore Math

Page 4:
a. Thursday and Friday
b. 8 degrees warmer

Page 9:
a. The duck laid 42 eggs in total.
b.

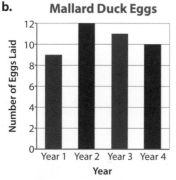

Mallard Duck Eggs

Page 10:

Day	Number of Sparrows Seen
Sunday	7
Saturday	6
Wednesday	4
Tuesday	3
Thursday	3
Friday	2
Monday	1

Page 16:

Dragonfly Nymphs Found

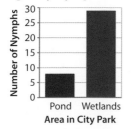

Page 26:
a. The flower garden and the wetlands
b. 10 more ducks
c. 40 ducks

Pages 28–29:

Problem-Solving Activity

a.

Day of the Week	Number of Birds
Monday	17
Tuesday	19
Wednesday	20
Thursday	18
Friday	22
Saturday	17
Sunday	16

b.

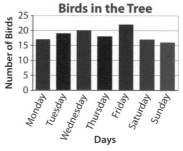

Birds in the Tree

c. Graph questions will vary.